Happy Valentine's Day, Emma!

by James Stevenson

Greenwillow Books New York

Watercolor paints were combined
with pen drawings for the
full-color illustrations.

Printed in Hong Kong by South China Printing Co.
First Edition
10 9 8 7 6 5 4 3 2 1

Library of Congress Cataloging-in-Publication Data
Stevenson, James (date)
Happy Valentine's Day, Emma!
Summary: Despite Dolores and Lavinia's
nasty cards, Emma the witch and her friends
have a wonderful Valentine's Day.
[1. Valentine's Day—Fiction.
2. Witches—Fiction.
3. Cartoons and comics]   I. Title.
PZ7.S84748Hap 1987   [E]   87-13
ISBN 0-688-07357-3
ISBN 0-688-07358-1 (lib. bdg.)